Matthew and Tall Rabbit Go Camping

By Susan Meyer

Illustrated by Amy Huntington

Camden, Maine

ISBN: 978-0-89272-769-8

Printed in China

5 4 3 2 1

Down East

Books, Magazine, Online
Camden, Maine
Book Orders: 800-685-7962
www.downeast.com
Distributed to the trade by National Book Network

Library of Congress Cataloging-in-Publication Data:
Meyer, Susan, 1960-
Matthew and Tall Rabbit : go camping / story by Susan Meyer ; illustrated by Amy Huntington.
p. cm.
Summary: Matthew and his parents go camping in the woods, and Matthew seeks to reassure his toy rabbit about the things that worry him.
ISBN 978-0-89272-769-8 (trade hardcover : alk. paper)
[1. Camping--Fiction. 2. Fear--Fiction. 3. Rabbits--Fiction. 4. Toys--Fiction.] I. Huntington, Amy, ill. II. Title. III. Title: Matthew and Tall Rabbit go camping.
PZ7.M571751Mat 2008
[E]--dc22

2007039497

For Ken and Hannah
— Susan

For Jake and Ande
— Amy

Matthew and Tall Rabbit had been waiting and waiting to go camping, but now that Mom was packing, Tall Rabbit was starting to look worried.

Matthew found Mom getting the sleeping bags down from the closet.

"Mom," said Matthew, "Tall Rabbit wants to know what we will do if we hear a lion roaring in the woods."

Mom smiled at Matthew. "There aren't any lions there," she said. "But if Tall Rabbit listens carefully with his big ears, he might hear loons calling on the lake. It is a beautiful, faraway sound."

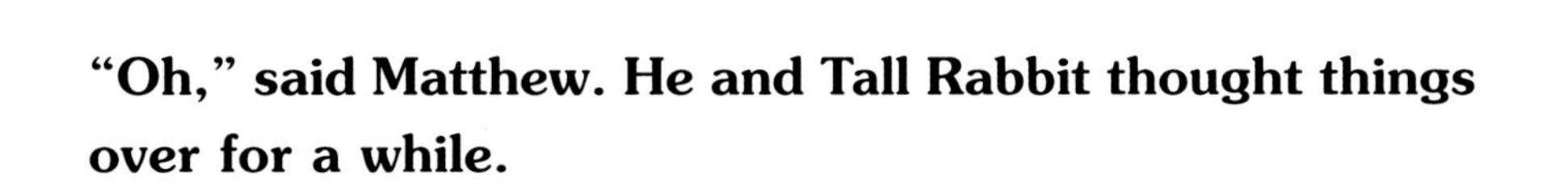

"Oh," said Matthew. He and Tall Rabbit thought things over for a while.

"Mom," said Matthew, "Tall Rabbit wonders if it will be cold outside at night."

"Yes, it will be. Tall Rabbit is right about that," answered Mom. "At night, we will all put on warm sweatshirts and sit around the campfire."

In the basement, Matthew found a bag of his outgrown baby clothes. There was a yellow sweatshirt in it that fit Tall Rabbit just right.

HIKING TRAILS

Dad was in the driveway putting the tent into the car.

"Dad," said Matthew, "Tall Rabbit wants to know if we can bring the nightlight when we go camping. He always watches it at night."

"No, Matthew, we can't bring the nightlight. There won't be anywhere to plug it in. But Tall Rabbit can look at the moon as he goes to sleep."

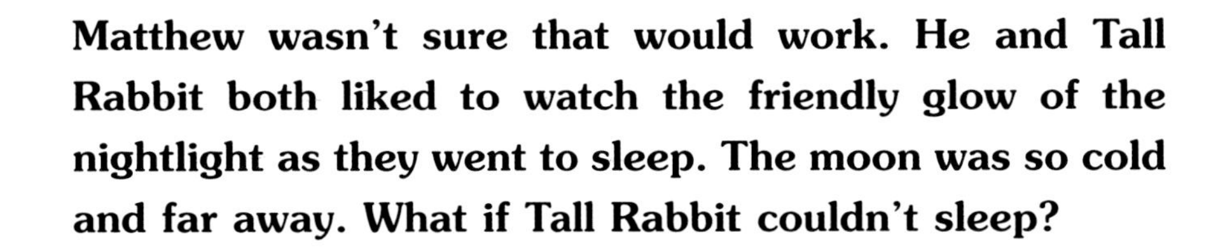

Matthew wasn't sure that would work. He and Tall Rabbit both liked to watch the friendly glow of the nightlight as they went to sleep. The moon was so cold and far away. What if Tall Rabbit couldn't sleep?

Matthew held Tall Rabbit close to comfort him on the long ride up to the lake.

When they got to the campground, there was a lot to do. Tall Rabbit sat on a stump and watched Matthew carry sleeping bags from the car while Mom and Dad put up the tent.

Dad showed Matthew how to use a big rock to bang in the stakes.

Then the tent fell down,

and Mom and Dad put it up again.

Matthew rolled out the three sleeping bags inside the tent, putting his sleeping bag in the middle. Matthew and Tall Rabbit lay down on Matthew's sleeping bag to try it out. Tall Rabbit thought the tent was very cozy, almost like a rabbit hole.

"Matthew," called Mom, "Can you gather some kindling and pinecones for the fire?"

The hotdogs Matthew and Mom and Dad cooked on sticks over the fire were the best thing Matthew had ever tasted. Matthew fed Tall Rabbit a piece. Tall Rabbit whispered in Matthew's ear that he still liked carrots best, but campfire hotdogs were the next best food.

"Time for bed now, Matthew," Dad announced. "Mom and I are going to sit out here by the fire for a while."

Mom took Matthew to the latrine in the woods. Matthew took as long as he could brushing his teeth at the cold-water sink outside, watching the last glow of the sunset over the lake. He gave Mom and Dad long goodnight kisses and hugs.

When he and Tall Rabbit crawled into the tent, it seemed different from before. The tent seemed to hold the darkness in, and it smelled funny, not like home.

"Don't be scared, Tall Rabbit," Matthew murmured. Together they lay in the sleeping bag and watched Mom and Dad through the open flap of the tent. The campfire crackled and glowed, but the sky got darker and darker.

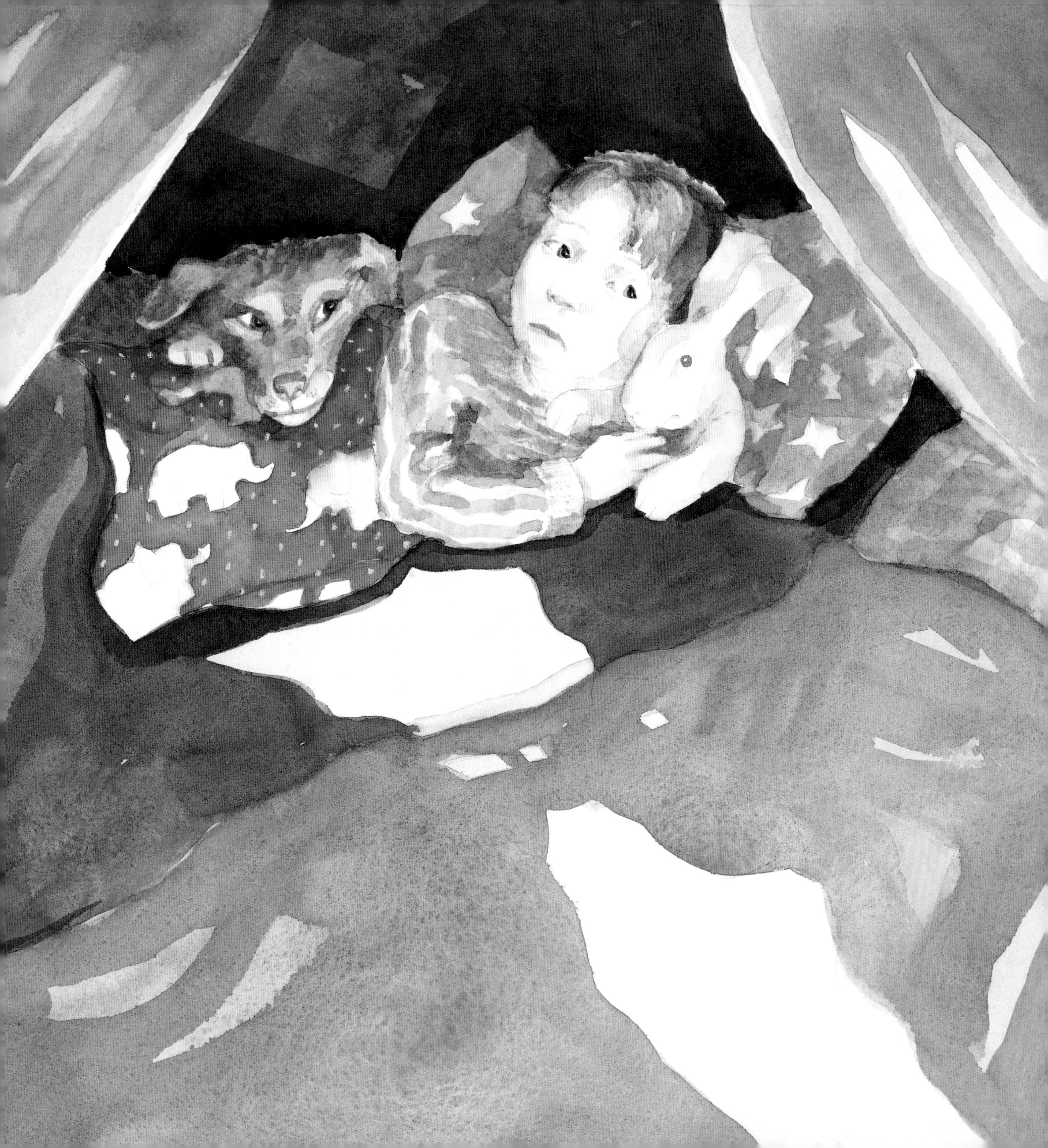

Matthew held Tall Rabbit tightly. A tiny light suddenly lit up near the opening of the tent, then went out. Then another glimmered and disappeared.

"Mom! What is that?" called Matthew.

Mom got up from her seat by the fire and came over.

"Those are fireflies, Matthew," she answered.
"Aren't they magical?"

"Fireflies!" whispered Matthew to Tall Rabbit.
"You don't have to worry now. They can be our nightlights!"

The fireflies fluttered and glimmered, in and out of the tent, making the night time friendly. Matthew and Tall Rabbit watched them and watched them until they both fell asleep.

·The End·